The Mask of Power

Trigger Happy
Targets
the Evil Kaos

GROSSET & DUNLAP
Penguin Young Readers Group
An Imprint of Penguin Random House LLC

Written by Cavan Scott
Illustrated by Dani Geremia—Beehive Illustration Agency

© 2016 ACTIVISION Publishing, Inc. SKYLANDERS UNIVERSE is a trademark
and ACTIVISION is a registered trademark of Activision Publishing, Inc.
All rights reserved. Published by Grosset & Dunlap, an imprint of
Penguin Random House LLC, 345 Hudson Street, New York, New York 10014.
GROSSET & DUNLAP is a trademark of Penguin Random House LLC.
Printed in the USA.

ISBN 978-1-101-99605-8   10 9 8 7 6 5 4 3 2 1

The Mask of Power

Trigger Happy
Targets
the Evil Kaos

by Onk Beakman

Grosset & Dunlap
An Imprint of Penguin Random House

About the Author

Onk Beakman knew he wanted to be a world-famous author from the moment he was hatched. In fact, the book-loving penguin was so excited that he wrote his first novel while still inside his egg (to this day, nobody is entirely sure where he got the tiny pencil and notebook from).

Growing up on the icy wastes of Skylands' Frozen Desert was difficult for a penguin who hated the cold. While his brothers plunged into the freezing waters, Onk could be found with his beak buried in a book and a pen clutched in his flippers.

Yet his life changed forever when a giant floating head appeared in the skies above the tundra. It was Kaos, attempting to melt the icecaps so he could get his grubby little hands on an ancient weapon buried beneath the snow.

Onk watched open-beaked as Spyro swept in and sent the evil Portal Master packing. From that day, Onk knew that he must chronicle the Skylanders' greatest adventures. He traveled the length and breadth of Skylands, collecting every tale he could find about Master Eon's brave champions.

Today, Onk writes from a shack on the beautiful sands of Blistering Beach with his two pet sea cucumbers.

Chapter One

Snake Attack!

Since you're reading this book, the chances are you've never had to fight a Water Viper. For this, you should count yourself very, very lucky.

Some of you may not even know what a Water Viper is. If that's the case, imagine a snake. One with a wriggly, muscular body and lots of scales. Oh, and long needlelike fangs, too.

The snake in your head is probably pretty scary, right? Like something out of a nightmare.

Well, a Water Viper is worse. Much worse.

First, take the snake you just imagined and make it the size of a house. Not a small house—a really big house.

Now, color its scales aqua-blue, and make them super-slimy. Finally, give your snake glowing red eyes and fangs as long as your arm. Actually, make them twice as long as your arm.

If you've done all that then, you're halfway to imagining just how insanely terrifying a Water Viper actually is. Fortunately for you, they don't exist in your world. They live in Skylands, the most magical place in all of creation. Here in Skylands, millions of trillions of gazillions of enchanted islands float in a bright blue sky. These islands are filled with amazing creatures as well as terrifying monsters. Water Vipers fall into the latter category.

Luckily for the people of Skylands, there is a band of heroes who fight monsters and other followers of The Darkness. These are the

Skylanders: courageous champions who will stop at nothing to keep Skylands safe from evil.

Courageous champions such as the three who heard a cry for help coming from Mabu Market and rushed to find a Water Viper attacking the timid Mabu who worked there.

"No gold, no glory!"

Trigger Happy was the first Skylander to leap from the Portal of Power, which had transported the three heroes to Mabu Market. He was a giggling gremlin, covered in rust-colored fur and with a ridiculously long tongue that lolled out of his permanently grinning mouth.

But his tongue wasn't the first thing people usually noticed about Trigger Happy. No, the first thing was that he was holding two massive golden guns.

Trigger Happy was the best shot in Skylands. In fact, he still is. He never misses, but his guns don't fire bullets or missiles; his shiny shooters fire gold coins. This is why people cheer when Trigger Happy appears and sends bad guys packing. Not only does he drive wrongdoers out of your hometown, he leaves so much gold ammo lying around that you'll be rich for the rest of your life.

Usually Trigger Happy likes to shoot first and answer questions later (most of the time he forgets to *ask* the questions at all). However, even he paused when he saw the state of Mabu Market. Trigger Happy had appeared on the top of a large market stall, but the rest of the place was in chaos. Most of the other booths were underwater. The entire market was completely flooded. Waterlogged Mabu struggled in the flood, bobbing among crates and pots in water that was as choppy and rough as any sea.

"But that's impossible," said a voice beside Trigger Happy. It was Food Fight, a Life Skylander. Like Trigger Happy, Food Fight carried a large cannon—but this one fired massive ripe tomatoes and other assorted

fruits and vegetables. As his name suggested, Food Fight didn't just play with his food—he fought with it!

A third figure materialized beside the others, dressed in jet-black armor that highlighted her burning red eyes.

"This doesn't make sense," said the newcomer, Smolderdash. "There isn't any water for miles. No lakes, no seas—nothing."

"That's right," agreed a monocle-wearing creature who was swimming toward them. It was Auric, a trader in magical artifacts and potions. He had worked with the Skylanders plenty of times, but now he needed their help. When he reached their perch, a shadow fell over them. Then he pointed at the sky and added, "But there is that!"

High in the air, a huge face loomed into view. It was connected to a long, scaly body. It was a Water Viper!

Before the Skylanders could react, the Water Viper opened its gigantic jaws and spewed a column of water right at them. Trigger Happy and the others leaped out of the way as water crashed into the market stall, smashing it to pieces.

This Water Viper had Skylanders on its menu!

Chapter Two

Water Fight

"Watch out!" Food Fight shouted as another burst of water blasted toward them—but his fellow Skylanders weren't going to end up as snake snacks today. Before Trigger Happy splashed into the floodwaters, he fired off a volley of super-shiny coins. They cut through the air, sunlight reflecting off their gleaming faces and dazzling the giant snake before the coins bounced off the monster's scaly skin.

The other Skylanders didn't waste time, either. Landing nimbly on a floating barrel, Smolderdash threw up her hands. Soon, a group of blazing Solar Orbs flew from her palms. The shining globes erupted into flames near the monster's head, confusing it even more. The beast flailed around, sending torrents of water everywhere.

Food Fight, meanwhile, was treading the choppy water, but that didn't stop him from sending a barrage of bright red tomatoes into the air. The fruit splattered against the snake's scales, smothering its skin in pulp and tomato juice. That gave the Life Skylander an idea.

"Hey, Smolder!" he yelled as Trigger Happy burst through the surface of the water beside him. "Feel like doing some cooking?"

Smolderdash grinned in reply. "I'm ready to turn up the heat if you are!"

While Trigger Happy continued dazzling the snake with his coins, Food Fight went into overdrive, covering the Viper's scaly hide with red sludge. Soon, it was impossible to see the snake's skin through all the tomato pulp.

"Over to you, Smolderdash. Old Snake Eyes is ripe for conquest!" Food Fight shouted to Smolderdash.

The Fire Skylander leaped from her barrel and threw herself toward the monster.

"Lighting the way!" she cried as her entire body began to glow like a miniature sun— even Trigger Happy and Food Fight had to protect their eyes from the fierce glare. But that was nothing compared to what happened to the Water Viper.

As Smolderdash flared, the tomato pulp

baked into a rock-hard shell that creaked as the monster desperately tried to wriggle free.

"Hey, Trigger Happy," Food Fight said, still squinting in the light. "Can you get me up high? It's pulping time!"

"Yeah, yeah," Trigger Happy jabbered, producing a giant pot of gold. "Stand on this!"

Food Fight did what he was told and leaped onto the gleaming cauldron, which was already vibrating beneath his feet. This wasn't any ordinary pot of gold—it was an *exploding* pot of gold.

"Pa-pa-POW!" Trigger Happy shrieked with glee as his golden grenade detonated, throwing Food Fight into the air. As he rocketed skyward, the Life Skylander blasted the Water Viper with flying fruit, covering its writhing body once again. The serpent was smothered from head to tail.

"Bake that snake!" Trigger Happy giggled wildly as Smolderdash did just that, sending a blinding flare up into the sky. By the time the glare died down, not only had the Water Viper been trapped inside a baked-tomato crust, but the floodwater had all but evaporated thanks to Smolderdash's heat. Steam rose from the damp ground as the Mabu fanned themselves in the sudden heat wave.

"We won, we won, we won!" Trigger Happy cheered, firing even more coins into the air in celebration.

Smolderdash turned to her friends and smiled, just as the solidified snake toppled over and crashed to the muddy ground, completely immobile. "We eclipse all others," she said.

Food Fight sniffed the air. "Mmmmm. Smell that? It kind of makes me hungry."

But further celebrations—and food—would have to wait. The victorious Skylanders spun around as a Portal opened behind them. A familiar figure emerged from the light.

"Spyro!" Trigger Happy exclaimed as the purple dragon landed in front of them. "What

are you doing here?"

"I've come to get the three of you," Spyro replied. "We're all needed back at the Citadel."

Even Trigger Happy's smile faltered. He'd never seen his friend look so worried. The Citadel was the Skylanders' base. It was home to the greatest Portal Master ever, Master Eon. It was Master Eon who had invited them all to be Skylanders in the first place, and they were all fiercely loyal to the old wizard.

"What's wrong?" Smolderdash asked.

"You'll see," Spyro said, leaping back into the Portal. "Just hurry."

Swapping concerned glances, the three remaining Skylanders followed the dragon, disappearing from sight before the Portal closed.

Mabu Market was suddenly very quiet. Auric the merchant wiped his glasses on a silk handkerchief and looked around at the carnage the defeated Water Viper had caused.

"Oh dear, oh dear," he muttered, slipping his glasses back onto his nose. "This will take forever to clean up."

At least his own stall didn't seem too badly damaged. Since some of his magical trinkets and potions were extremely dangerous, Auric kept them safely under lock and key in a tall ornate cabinet. Sure enough, when he traipsed through the mud to check, the wooden cupboard was still there, shut tight.

But when Auric unlocked the doors, just to make sure, he gasped in shock and dismay. His cabinet of amazing curiosities was completely empty. Someone had stolen all of his stuff!

Chapter Three

The Book of Power

"Is this about the Mask of Power?" Trigger Happy asked Spyro as they appeared in the Citadel's echoey Portal Chamber. "Is it, is it, is it?"

"I hope not," Food Fight said glumly. "That thing gives me the creeps."

"That's what it's supposed to do," pointed out Smolderdash.

But the problem with the Mask of Power was that no one knew exactly what it was supposed to do, or how it worked.

For a while now, Kaos, the Skylanders' archenemy and all-around bad guy, had been trying to find the fragments of the mysterious ancient mask. It originally belonged to a tyrant called King Nefarion, and it was said to make its wearer all-powerful. No wonder Kaos wanted to get his exceptionally grubby hands on it. Kaos had two ambitions in life:

1) To conquer Skylands.

2) To find a cure for his baldness.

For all the Skylanders knew, the Mask of Power would allow him to do both. What was worse was that Kaos already had most of the pieces—although the Fire and Life segments were safely locked away at the heart of Master Eon's Citadel. There was still one piece missing—the fragment of the mask associated with the Magic Element—and it was a race against time to see who would get it first.

"Master Eon's waiting," said Spyro, leading his friends down a long stone corridor and into the Citadel library. Master Eon stood beside an elaborate podium, his long beard looking whiter than ever. There were heavy shadows beneath his usually bright eyes, as well. The search for the mask was having a profound effect on the Portal Master, making him appear frailer than ever.

He looked up as the Skylanders ran into the library.

"Ah, there you are," Master Eon said, his voice deep and strong despite his appearance. "And the Water Viper?"

"Baked to perfection." Trigger Happy giggled. A look of confusion passed over the Portal Master's face, but he shook it off and moved on to more pressing matters. Gravely, he turned back to the book on the stand.

"As you can see, my Skylanders," the Portal Master began, "the Book of Power is still bearing bad tidings."

The Skylanders followed his gaze, looking at the pictures on the large book's yellowing pages. This was no ordinary book. It predicted when the next fragment of the mask would appear; unfortunately, it only spoke in pictures, which made its contents more of a riddle than any text could ever be.

The current picture was all too clear, however. It showed Kaos wearing the Mask of Power while the Skylanders cowered at his feet. It was the book's prediction of what was to come. Trigger Happy felt like shooting a hole in the middle of the picture with an extra-large gold coin.

"So, what about the final segment?" Food Fight asked. "Has it given us any clues?"

"That is why I had Spyro bring you back," Master Eon said, raising a weary hand toward the book. "Book of Power, reveal to me the location of the Magic fragment. Show me where it is."

A wind blew through the library, turning the pages of the book in front of their eyes. The book rested open on an empty spread before lines started appearing across the paper as if drawn by an invisible hand. The lines swept this way and that, forming a perfect picture of . . .

"A sheep?" Spyro said, underwhelmed. "Well, I guess each segment of the mask is disguised as something that is the complete opposite of its power."

"Yeah, and sheep sure fit the bill. They're the most boring, un-magical creatures in Skylands," Food Fight pointed out.

Master Eon frowned. "No creature is boring," he retorted. "From the smallest ant to the largest dragon, all are worthy of protection, and all have a spark of magic within their souls—especially here in Skylands."

Food Fight looked embarrassed. "Sorry," he said, only to feel Master Eon's hand on his shoulder. He glanced up to see the Portal Master smiling kindly down at him.

"No, I am sorry. I was wrong to snap. These are"—he paused, searching for the right word—"troubling times. We must remember to help one another, young or old."

Trigger Happy still wasn't convinced, though. He was bouncing up and down to get a closer look at the sheep.

"But there are millions of sheep across Skylands," he said. "How do we know which one is the right one—huh, huh, huh?"

Trigger Happy always liked saying things three times. It was one of his hobbies. That and shooting things, of course.

"Very good point," Master Eon said, standing up a little straighter. "Book, where is this sheep? Tell me!"

The sheep shrank down on the page as a new image appeared: a tall, craggy mountain covered in what looked like fluffy white clouds. Master Eon tore the page from the book and gave it to the Skylanders.

"Those aren't clouds," Smolderdash said as she took a closer look. "That's Wool Mountain."

"I've been there," shouted Spyro, immediately running for the doors. "We'll find the fragment in no time. Come on, guys!"

With a cheer, the other Skylanders chased after the dragon, who was heading back to the Portal Room. Master Eon chuckled as he watched them go. His Skylanders were always so full of enthusiasm, no matter how dark the situation. *And long may it continue,* he said to himself.

However, even as he listened to the Skylanders' excited cries, Master Eon failed to notice something very strange. Behind him, at the back of the library, stood a small wooden chair. It seemed normal enough until, once Master Eon's back was turned, it started to move. Slowly, quietly, the wooden stool crept off by itself and scurried out of the room.

Chapter Four

Wool Mountain

"Heh, how hard can it be to find one sheep?" Food Fight said as the Skylanders took the Portal to Wool Mountain.

Trigger Happy's yellow eyes widened as he took in the scene in front of them. "Pretty hard—yeah, yeah, yeah."

He wasn't wrong. The mountainside was covered in sheep—sheep to the left, sheep to the right, sheep up high, and sheep down below.

"It's fine," insisted Spyro, turning to face Smolderdash. "Have you got the piece of paper Master Eon gave us?"

The Fire Skylander held out a single page of brittle parchment. "This is from the Book of Power itself," she said. "It will glow once we get close to the fragment, which is disguised as one of these sheep."

Spyro told her to rip the paper into four pieces. Once that was done, Smolderdash gave a piece of it to each of them.

"Let's spread out," Spyro said. "We've got a lot of sheep to check."

He wasn't wrong. After an hour, the Skylanders were beginning to hope that they would never see another fleece or hear another bleat ever again.

"Could the book be, you know, wrong?" asked Food Fight, checking his 284,829th sheep.

"It hasn't been so far," pointed out Spyro, pressing his paper against an uninterested sheep's wooly back and frowning as the paper stubbornly refused to glow.

"It's definitely here," jabbered Trigger Happy, looking into the sky.

"How can you tell?" asked Food Fight.

"Because *he's* here!" replied the Tech Skylander.

"Who?" asked Smolderdash. She gazed up to where Trigger Happy was looking and glowered at what she saw. "Oh, him!"

Something had appeared in the sky. Something big. Something ugly. Something bald. And something exceptionally evil.

"Kaos!" Spyro hissed through clenched fangs.

"Yes, it is I, KAOOOOS!" the evil Portal Master roared down at them from on high. Or rather, his giant floating head roared.

This was one of Kaos's latest tricks. In reality, the Skylanders' archenemy was a small, weedy so-and-so. He had a scrawny body, a distinct lack of hair, and even less personal hygiene. At first glance you could be forgiven for dismissing him out of hand, but that would be a mistake. Despite his appearance, Kaos was one of the most dangerous and powerful beings in Skylands, and really mean to boot.

To make sure everyone feared him, he had started projecting a huge, scary version of his head into the sky. In all honesty, it was far more impressive than his real head—but Spyro knew it was all a trick.

"What are you doing here?" Spyro snarled, flying up to face the giant head.

"What do you think, dragonfly?" Kaos sneered. "I'm here to claim what is rightfully mine. The Mask of POWER!"

On the ground, Food Fight stared at the giant face. "I don't get it. How did he know we'd turnip here? The Magic segment's location was supposed to be secret!"

Kaos's giant face swiveled to look down at the Life Skylander. "Well, that's for me to know, fruit face, and for you to NEVER find out."

"We won't let you have it," Spyro promised.

"Yeah, yeah, yeah!" Trigger Happy agreed. "We win! Always!"

Kaos snorted. "You won't this time, SKYLOSERS! I summon my terrible Trolls in their flying machines!" He paused, frowning. "No, that doesn't sound right. Let's try again. I summon my terrible Trolls in their flying machines OF DOOOOOM! Yes, that's much better."

As Kaos babbled, the air filled with the sound of rattling engines and propeller blades. Six Troll fighter planes swept around Kaos's head. They looked incredibly rickety, with more wings than they really needed and dozens of Trolls crammed into each cockpit. They were also packed with all kinds of weapons.

Kaos unleashed his most maniacal laugh yet as the planes swooped down, firing at the Skylanders on the ground, guns blazing. And these were no ordinary guns. They fired Chompies—little green critters with big gnashing teeth.

"Protect the sheep!" Spyro roared. "Any of them might be the segment!"

"Way ahead of you, Spyro," Food Fight shouted back, raising his fruit cannon. "Eat my veggies!"

The Life Skylander squeezed his trigger, and a volley of zucchini hit the first Troll Fighter right in the propeller. The machine exploded, sending Trolls and Chompies alike crashing to the ground.

Food Fight didn't have time to celebrate, however. Another plane was coming straight for him, sweeping low over the sheep to try to take the Life Skylander out of the battle.

Chapter Five

The Magic Segment

Food Fight noticed the incoming plane just a little too late. He turned to aim his weapon, but didn't have time to target the Trolls.

Luckily, he wasn't on his own.

"You're not so bright," Smolderdash said with a grin. She jumped to her friend's aid, a flaming whip appearing in her hand. "Unlike me!"

Shrieking, the Trolls tried to pull up, but it was too late. Smolderdash's whip raked across the plane's body, cutting the flying machine in two.

"NOOOOO!" screamed Kaos from above. "What are you doing, FOOLS? *You* should be destroying *them,* not the other way around!"

"It's four against four now," Spyro shouted as he swooped down toward his fellow Skylanders. "Hey, Trigger Happy! Want to go for a spin?"

"Yeah, yeah, yeah!" Trigger Happy yelled back, immediately catching Spyro's drift. Looking up at the purple dragon, he stuck out his tongue—but he wasn't being rude. When Trigger Happy sticks out his tongue, he REALLY sticks out his tongue. It shot up into the air, and Spyro grabbed it. At once, the super-stretchy licker snapped back to its normal length like an elastic band, propelling Trigger Happy up toward his friend. Flipping over, the Tech Skylander landed on Spyro's scaly back.

"Locked and loaded!" Trigger Happy cried with delight as Spyro soared toward the nearest flying machine.

"Let's go Troll hunting!" the dragon cheered as Trigger Happy gleefully fired gold coins into the air.

The Trolls in the plane hadn't even noticed that Spyro and Trigger Happy were coming. They had locked on to Smolderdash and were firing Chompy after Chompy at the Fire Skylander. Not that it mattered. Spyro swooped low, and Trigger Happy blew the plane to bits with an exploding golden safe. Oh yes, Trigger Happy had more than just golden coins in his arsenal.

As the flying machine smashed into the ground, Spyro swept over to Smolderdash. "Smolderdash," the dragon shouted down as he banked in the air. "You and Food Fight find the sheep. We'll take care of the Trolls."

"Yeah, take care," Trigger Happy repeated merrily. "Pow! Pow! Pow!"

Smolderdash and Food Fight went to work, rushing their way through the sheep as the battle raged in the sky above them.

Soon the fourth flying machine had found itself torched by Spyro's fiery breath, while the fifth was downed by more of Trigger Happy's never-ending supply of ammo.

Now there was only one plane left to defeat.

"Where is it?" said Spyro, glancing around. The Troll fighter was nowhere to be seen.

Suddenly, Trigger Happy bounced up and down on Spyro's back. "Up, up, up!" the gremlin gabbled.

Spyro looked up to see the remaining fighter plane screaming down right on top of them.

"Hold on!" he shouted, coming to an abrupt halt in the air. Chompies streamed around them, the plane getting nearer by the second. "And hold your fire, too," Spyro added.

Trigger Happy frowned. Stop firing? Had Spyro gone crazy? The plummeting plane was getting dangerously close. Perhaps one of those Chompies had hit the dragon a bit too hard on his horned head.

But, right at the last moment, Spyro darted out of the way with a flap of his leathery wings.

The pilot's eyes went as wide as dinner plates when he realized the Troll fighter was diving too fast. There was no way it could pull up in time . . . BOOOOOOOOOOM!

The sound of the explosion echoed across the mountainside.

"Oh yeah!" Spyro cheered. "This is one dragon who can never be beaten. And the same goes for you, Trigger Happy!"

Trigger Happy's only response was to fire more coins into the air, even though all of the

Trolls had been totally defeated. "Pow, pow, POW!"

"Well, you may have won the battle, SKYBLUNDERERS," Kaos shouted, obviously trying to hide his disappointment, "but you'll never find the last segment of the mask!"

"Is that so, potato head?" shouted a voice from below. Spyro looked down to see Food Fight standing triumphantly next to a confused-looking sheep. Even better, the scrap of paper from the Book of Power was glowing brighter than Smolderdash.

"Well done, Food Fight!" Spyro said, dropping down as Trigger Happy vaulted off his back. Defiantly, the purple dragon glared up at Kaos. "What do you say to that, Kaos? Who's the loser now?"

The Skylanders dropped into defensive poses, each ready for whatever horror Kaos was going to unleash next. One thing was certain: The evil Portal Master wouldn't give up without a fight.

"You found it," Kaos wailed, his lip wobbling. "I'm DOOOOOOOOMED!"

"You are?" Smolderdash asked, completely bewildered.

"Please don't hurt me," Kaos pleaded, his head shrinking in front of their amazed eyes. "I'm not worth it! You have won and I have lost—FOREVER!"

"This is weird," Food Fight muttered. "What's the sly spud up to?"

Spyro had to agree. He'd never seen Kaos like this.

The Portal Master's giant head wasn't even that giant anymore. It had almost shrunk down to its normal size.

"Farewell, Skylanders," he said, bawling. "After all our battles, it appears that the only fool in Skylands is KAOOOOOOOS! You will never hear of me again."

With a rather disappointing flash of light, the Portal Master was gone.

The Skylanders stood for a second, still expecting an attack, but the only sound on Wool Mountain was the bleating of a thousand sheep.

"Did that just happen?" asked Food Fight.

Spyro shrugged in answer. Could it be that, after all this time, Kaos had just admitted defeat?

Chapter Six

Safe and Sound

"Well done, my Skylanders," Master Eon said as Spyro, Trigger Happy, and the others appeared on the Portal of Power along with an increasingly befuddled-looking sheep.

"Aaaaaaaaaaaaargh!" yelped a small bespectacled Mabu standing beside the Portal Master. "What do you think you're doing bringing that monstrosity here? Get it out! Get it out, now!"

This was Hugo, Master Eon's timid assistant and librarian. For reasons known only to himself, Hugo had a morbid fear of sheep and was forever trying his best to convince the Skylanders that the woolly creatures were plotting to take over the entire universe. The appearance of one inside the Citadel was too much for him to bear.

"Calm down, Hugo," Master Eon said, before turning his attention back to Spyro. "Is this the segment?"

Spyro held up his glowing scrap of paper. "I think so."

Without another word, Master Eon raised his arms. The Portal Room crackled with energy as his magic started to build.

"Reveal yourself, last fragment of the mask," the Portal Master commanded. At once, the sheep stopped chewing, and a blank expression fell across its already distracted features. As the Skylanders watched—and Hugo cowered behind Eon's robes—the animal floated into the air and started spinning around and around and around and around.

Spyro could feel his scales tingling as the

sheep spun so fast it became a woolly blur and then blazed with light. Even Smolderdash had to turn away, and when they looked back the sheep was gone, replaced with a wooden fragment of mask.

"Behold the Magic segment," Master Eon said as the fragment floated over to land in his open hand.

"Thank goodness for that." Hugo sighed, pleased that the sheep was gone—oh, and glad that Kaos hadn't taken the last segment of the Mask of Power, of course.

Master Eon turned to the small Mabu. "Hugo, would you place this in the safe with the other fragments?"

"Of course," Hugo said, trying to make himself sound as important as possible. "It will be a pleasure."

"The sooner that thing's locked up, the better," Food Fight added. "Away from Kaos, that is."

"Do you think he meant what he said?"

asked Smolderdash. "About being defeated, I mean."

Spyro frowned. "I'm not sure. He sounded sincere . . ."

"But when have we ever trusted him before, eh, eh, eh?" Trigger Happy pointed out.

"Well, better to be safe than sorry," said Hugo, scurrying off. "Do you see what I did there? Better to be *safe*? As in, *I'm putting this in a safe.*"

Master Eon rolled his eyes. "Yes, yes, very funny. Now hurry up, will you?"

But Hugo was already gone.

The safe was in the heart of the Citadel library, between the Ancient Arkeyan History section and Advanced Basket Weaving. It was definitely the safest place for it, too. Only Hugo could find his way around the maze of bookshelves and cabinets. He'd worked here his whole life, cataloging Master Eon's vast collection of books—a collection, it was said, that was rivaled only by the legendary Eternal Archive of the Warrior Librarians.

The library was so big that Master Eon had installed mini Portals to help Hugo jump between departments quickly—otherwise he could spend months trudging through the dusty bookshelves.

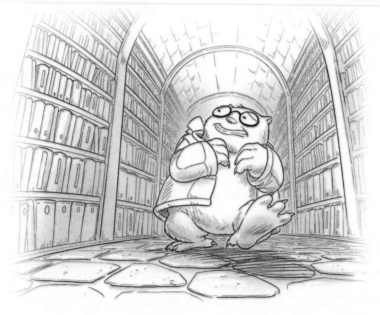

As he waddled toward the safe, Hugo hummed a tune, not because he was happy, but because he was nervous. Ever since he'd left the Portal Room, he had felt sure that he was being followed. It was a ridiculous feeling, he knew. No one could get into the Citadel, except for the Skylanders, of course, and none of them would follow him this far into the library—even for a joke. Some Skylanders, such as Trigger Happy, often played pranks on the studious librarian. The gremlin was still giggling about the time he had hidden a sheep in a barrel of Hugo's favorite cookies. Hugo had settled down for some hot chocolate and a cookie and *BAAAAAAA!* The woolly beast had popped out like a jack-in-the-box. You could probably have heard Hugo's scream in the Outlands.

But this was different. Even Trigger Happy wouldn't play a trick on him today, not when he was carrying the last segment of the mask.

And yet, every now and then, Hugo thought he could hear tiny feet running after him. The Mabu stopped and looked around. There was no one there. The corridor behind him was empty, except for a big red book that was just lying on the floor. Hugo clicked his tongue and padded over to the book, slotting it back onto a shelf.

"A place for everything, and everything in its place," he muttered to himself, his voice sounding very small in the echoey hallway.

Hugo continued on his way, turning right at the Legendary Treasures collection, when he heard the noise again. Those feet chasing after him.

"Now, look here . . . ," he said, whirling around. But once again he was alone. All alone, except for a large red book lying on the floor. That couldn't be right, could it? Surely he would have noticed another book lying on the floor as he hurried past, and besides, it was a bit of a coincidence, wasn't it? Two red books out of place?

Cautiously, Hugo walked up to the book

and tapped it with his foot. No, it couldn't be the same book. That was silly. Pushing his glasses up his nose, he made a decision. "I'll put the segment into the safe and then come back and find where this book should be. Yes, that's what I'll do."

But this time Hugo ran along the corridors. He was puffing and panting by the time he reached the safe. It was carved out of magical stone, and was impossible to open without a special code. Breathing heavily, Hugo reached forward and started turning the dial on the safe door, entering the combination that only he and Master Eon knew.

Fourteen, ten, twenty, eleven . . .

Hugo's ears twitched as he heard something move behind him, but he ignored the noise.

. . . twelve, twenty, ten, nineteen . . .

The noise was getting louder now. It was definitely the pattering of feet against the flagstones. Hugo rushed through the final

digits of the complicated combination.

   . . . twelve, ten, twenty, thirteen.

The lock clanged open, and something roared behind Hugo. Startled, he looked over his shoulder to see the red book running straight toward him on little red legs.

"No!" Hugo squealed, flattening his back against the safe and clutching the segment to his chest. "That's not possible."

But it wasn't as impossible as what happened next. As the book sprinted forward, it started to change. Its legs grew thicker, and muscular arms sprang from its covers. The book doubled in size, and then quadrupled. The red limbs became green. A head appeared on newly formed broad shoulders. The head had a flattened snout, beady eyes, and a leering mouth full of sharp teeth. By the time Hugo screamed for help, the book had transformed into a charging Goliath Drow, with a golden pendant sparkling around its bulging neck.

In the Portal Room, the Skylanders had been distracted by a call from the Portal of Power itself. Master Eon waved his hand, and Auric the trader appeared at the center of the Portal.

"Oh, Master Eon, thank you for seeing me," the Mabu said, stepping down toward the Portal Master.

"What's the problem?" asked Food Fight. "The Water Viper causing trouble again?"

"Oh, no, no, no," Auric said, wringing his hands. "That beastie slunk away almost as soon as your tomato crust finally crumbled."

"Then what is it?" Spyro asked.

"My cabinet of curiosities," Auric said. "Someone broke into it during the Water Viper attack."

"You mean the cabinet where you keep

your potions?" Smolderdash asked.

"And my magical artifacts, too," Auric replied. "But it's okay. I found them all thrown away not far from the market. All except one."

Before anyone could ask the market trader which artifact was missing, a cry cut through the stillness.

"HEEEEEEEEELP!"

It was faint, but there was no mistaking the voice.

"That's Hugo!" Spyro said.

"Quick," Master Eon urged. "To the safe."

The Skylanders raced through the library, following Eon. No one would have expected that the old man could move so quickly, but the situation was grim. If something had happened to Hugo before he could deposit the last segment of the Mask of Power into the safe . . .

"Can't you slow down?" Auric wheezed. He was chasing after them, not wanting to be left alone in the Portal Room.

"No time!" replied Trigger Happy. "Gotta go, go, go!"

"There's the safe!" shouted Spyro as they reached the stone stronghold.

"It's locked," said Master Eon. "Thank goodness."

"But where's the little pipsqueak?" asked Food Fight.

"I wonder," Master Eon said, leaning over and spinning the dial. It clicked and whirred as he entered the combination, and the door swung open to reveal . . .

"A sheep?" said Spyro in amazement.

A sheep was crammed into the safe, and a scared-looking sheep at that. Its knees knocked and its wool trembled as it stared at

them with wide, wet eyes.

"What's that hanging around its neck?" Smolderdash asked. Auric bustled through, pushing the Skylanders aside.

"It's my missing artifact," the trader said grimly. "The Shape-Shifting Sapphire Amulet. Absolutely priceless and terribly powerful."

Auric reached forward and gently plucked the necklace from around the sheep's neck. No sooner was it back in his hands than the sheep started to transform into a familiar, trembling figure.

"Hugo!" Master Eon spluttered in alarm. "Who did this to you, old friend?"

"I-i-it was a D-D-Drow," Hugo said, still cringing in the safe. "It t-t-took the segments and left th-th-this."

The Mabu reached out a shaking hand, giving the Portal Master a note. Master Eon read it and groaned softly.

"What does it say, Master Eon?" Spyro

asked. The wizard passed the paper to the dragon.

Spyro's eyes narrowed as he read the spidery writing.

Dear Skylosers,

Thank you for keeping the last two segments safe for me.

See you when I take over Skylands!

Lots of love,

Your archenemy,

Kaos the All-Powerful

XX

P.S. You are DOOOOOOOOOOMED,

etc., etc.!

Chapter Seven

Kaos's Kastle

Spyro bounded into the Portal Room, where the other Skylanders were waiting for him. Smolderdash had already generated some Solar Orbs, while Food Fight was checking the sights of his fruit cannon. Trigger Happy, meanwhile, was firing coins into the air, too excited to relax his trigger finger. This was going to be their biggest battle yet—and they weren't alone.

The Portal Room was packed with many of the Skylanders who had led quests to find the segments of the Mask of Power—Gill Grunt, Lightning Rod, Cynder, Terrafin, Stump

Smash, and others—all waiting for Master Eon to give the word. The air in the room was electric (and that wasn't just because of Zap the Water dragon).

"Are we leaving?" Trigger Happy asked. "Are we? Are we? Are we?"

Spyro was about to answer when a voice boomed from behind him.

"Yes, my Skylanders." Master Eon swept

into the vast chamber. "Today the fate of Skylands rests in your hands. Maybe the fate of the entire universe. I do not have to remind you that if Kaos conquers Skylands, he will have access to everywhere else, too. Nowhere will be safe."

"Then what are we waiting for?" asked Food Fight. "Lettuce teach the creep a lesson!"

"Yeah," added Terrafin the dirt shark.

"And get the five dollars he owes me, too!"

"Whatever we do," Spyro said, throwing open his wings and hovering in the air, "we work together. We aren't completely sure what powers Kaos will receive from the mask, but none of us will be able to defeat him alone. We are Skylanders. We fight together, right?"

"Right!" chorused the Skylanders.

Master Eon nodded his approval as he walked toward the Portal of Power. As he approached, the ancient symbols carved into the stone started to glow. He stopped, thrust his staff into the air, and was bathed in light as the surface of the Portal burst into life.

Gravely, he turned to the Skylanders. "I have opened a Portal to Kaos's Kastle. Be warned. His minions will be everywhere. Trolls. Drow. Maybe even worse."

"We'll stop him, Master Eon," Spyro said, swooping close. "You can rely on us."

Master Eon smiled. "Of course I can, Spyro. Of that I have no doubt."

"Are we ready?" the dragon called over his shoulder.

"Yeah, yeah, yeah!" shouted Trigger Happy, hopping up and down as the other Skylanders cheered and whooped. They were ready for anything.

"Then it's showtime!" Spyro yelled, before plunging into the Portal's light.

Kaos's Kastle suited its owner down to the ground. It positively reeked of evil. Floating on an evil island, it was a cluster of evil towers and evil battlements. Even the flowers in the ornamental gardens looked evil. No birds sang and no insects chirped. The air felt cold and clammy, as if no warmth was allowed.

And then there were the statues—lots and lots of statues. Kaos had always liked looking at statues of himself. In fact, his first attempt at conquering Skylands had basically involved scattering golden statues of himself all over the place. He had hoped that the people of Skylands would see them all and simply assume that he must be in charge.

It didn't work. The locals promptly pulled down each and every one of the eyesores, breaking them up to make rock gardens.

Needless to say, Kaos wasn't happy.

That hadn't stopped him from trying again, though. Indeed, according to Professor

P. Grungally, noted author of *Skylands and Why Bad Types Want to Conquer It* (Vol. 1–3½), Kaos has tried to take over Skylands approximately 1,839.7 times—sometimes twice before he's even had breakfast.

But Spyro wasn't concerned about any of that as he burst out of Master Eon's Portal. Not today. The purple dragon, who was once again carrying Trigger Happy on his back, was only focused on the task at hand: getting the Mask of Power away from Kaos before the evil Portal Master could start some serious trouble.

"Coming through!" Trigger Happy yelled as they appeared high in the sky above the Kastle. The other Skylanders appeared behind them. The ones who couldn't fly were held aloft by clouds controlled by Lightning Rod the Storm Titan. The ancestral home of the Kaos family loomed beneath them, its ramparts bristling with cannons and Troll troops. And that wasn't the worst of it.

"Drow Zeppelins!" Smolderdash yelled, pointing at three airships racing to meet them.

"They knew we were coming!" added Food Fight, ready to bombard the dark elves' flying machines with fruits and veggies.

"Of course they did," Spyro shouted back. "Kaos knew we wouldn't give up that easily. Are you all fired up, Skylanders?"

As one, the Skylanders cheered, "Yes!"

"Then adventure calls!" Spyro cried, swooping into battle.

The zeppelins had already started firing. Cannonballs zoomed up toward the attacking Skylanders.

"Is that the best you've got?" shouted Terrafin, punching one of the cannonballs away as if it was a beach ball, while Gill Grunt weaved in and out of the onslaught using his water pack.

Ahead of them all, riding on the back of Cynder, Smolderdash created Solar Orb after Solar Orb, splitting each orb into two with

her flame whip. Fireballs rained down on the enemy airships, the first finding its target and igniting the gas in the zeppelin's balloon.

"That's the spirit!" Cynder cheered as Smolderdash turned her attention toward the second balloon.

"Spyro, look!" Lightning Rod boomed, throwing up a muscular blue arm. "The fiends have reinforcements on the way."

Sure enough, an entire armada of Drow

Zeppelins was on the horizon. And they were coming in fast.

Even Spyro gasped at the sight. "I've never seen so many."

"The more the merrier." Trigger Happy giggled. "Pow, pow, pow!"

"But we need to get down to the Kastle," Spyro reminded him.

"Why didn't you say so?" Trigger Happy shrieked. Without another word, he leaped from Spyro's back and went into a free fall. The Tech Skylander plummeted toward the Kastle's ramparts, firing coins all the way.

"Trigger Happy!" Spyro yelled as Lightning Rod roared with laughter beside him.

"He always jumps in headfirst, that one," Lightning Rod bellowed. "He's almost as brave as me!"

"You go after him, Spyro," Cynder said, coming up alongside Lightning Rod. "We can handle the Drow, right, guys?"

The other Skylanders agreed readily; Smolderdash and Food Fight volunteered to go with Spyro.

"I want to fruit-punch Kaos right in the kisser," Food Fight said, leaping from his cloud onto Spyro's back, while Smolderdash jumped after Trigger Happy.

"Good luck!" Spyro said as he went into a dive, screaming after the Fire Skylander.

"Luck?" Lightning Rod scoffed. "It's the Drow that should be worried!" With a hearty chuckle, the Storm Titan clapped his huge hands together, summoning a thunderstorm in the skies around them. "Time to issue an extreme weather warning!"

"Yeah!" shouted Cynder. "Volts and lightning!"

As the storm—and the battle—raged overhead, Trigger Happy had already landed outside the main gates and was having a whale of a time dealing with Troll attacks from all angles. There were Trolls wielding wrenches, Trolls lobbing exploding barrels, and Trolls piloting Chompy-spewing tanks.

Trigger Happy didn't mind. More Trolls meant more targets, and more targets meant more fun!

"Eat gold!" he yelled at the advancing army, not even noticing Smolderdash landing gracefully beside him. He soon noticed her Solar Orbs cutting through the Kastle guards, though!

Above them, Spyro joined the fray, his fiery breath flaring as Food Fight somersaulted from the dragon's back to land alongside his fellow Skylanders. The four heroes were hideously outnumbered, but the Trolls didn't stand a chance. Soon the Trolls were covered in tomato pulp, being butted by Spyro's horns, cowering beneath a shower of coins, or watching helplessly as Smolderdash melted the weapons from their hands.

Trigger Happy looked up at the huge wooden doors that blocked their entrance to the Kastle. "Shall I blast 'em?"

"Go for it," Spyro said, flipping a Troll into the air with a flick of his horns.

"I'll help light the way!" shouted Smolderdash, generating a trio of Solar Orbs. "After you, Trigger Happy!"

As Spyro and Food Fight held back the Trolls, Trigger Happy and Smolderdash stood shoulder to shoulder and fired. Coins rattled against the wood of the door, while Solar Orbs attempted to melt the ornate metal hinges. "They must be thicker than they look," said Trigger Happy when the doors stubbornly refused to be smashed into smithereens. "Time to get a bigger trigger."

Smolderdash watched in awe as one of Trigger Happy's guns started to change. The barrel of one split open to reveal a large golden missile that grew and grew and grew until it was four times the size of Trigger Happy himself. The gremlin heaved the gun into the air and fired. The missile streaked up before looping over behind them and flying close to the ground to aim itself right at the door.

Smolderdash took a step back, but Trigger Happy jumped onto the speeding missile, straddling it like a bronco as it flew by.

"Rocket ride!" He laughed as the missile crashed into the massive double doors and exploded.

BOOM!

Chapter Eight

The Voice of Kaos!

Smolderdash coughed as the smoke cleared.

"Trigger Happy?" she called out, worried about her friend. Not that she should have been concerned. The dust settled to reveal the Tech Skylander rolling around on his back and giggling his head off. If it wasn't for the slightly singed tips of his ears, you'd never have guessed he had just been in the heart of an explosion.

"What a ride!" he whooped, flipping back over onto his feet.

Smolderdash was less positive. "The doors are still standing," she said with a groan.

Not only that, they looked completely unscathed.

"We should try again," said Spyro, whacking a Troll with his tail. "Perhaps if we concentrate all our firepower . . ."

"Yeah, but what about these Trolls?" said Food Fight. "There's even more than before."

"We could call the others for help," Smolderdash suggested, but a quick glance up at the battle in the sky told them that Lightning Rod and the others still had their hands full with the Drow.

"No, it's up to us!" said Spyro. "For Master Eon . . ."

"And Skylands," added Trigger Happy, his golden guns back in his hands.

But then something strange happened. Actually, it was something downright peculiar. One second the Skylanders were besieged by Trolls, and the next . . .

WHUMPH! WHUMPH! WHUMPH! WHUMPH!

One by one, the Trolls disappeared. Above them, the sound of cannon fire suddenly ceased as the Drow Zeppelins broke formation and zoomed away.

"Where are those pea-brains going?" Food Fight asked. Before anyone could answer, the giant doors of the Kastle creaked open by themselves.

Lightning Rod, Cynder, and the rest of the Skylanders dropped down to land beside Spyro as he peered into the gloomy Kastle interior.

"What happened?" asked Gill Grunt.

"I've no idea," said Spyro. "But I don't like it."

"Do you think it's a trap?" asked Smolderdash.

"This is Kaos we're dealing with," Spyro replied. "What do you think?"

"I think we should proceed with caution," said Lightning Rod. "Not that I'm worried, you understand. I'm just thinking of you guys!"

Spyro smirked at the Storm Titan's

bravado. Lightning Rod always liked to remind everyone that he was amazing, but this time the look of concern on his noble features was obvious.

"We'll be careful." Spyro nodded. "All of us!"

"Yeah, careful," whooped Trigger Happy, who then ran into the Kastle before anyone could stop him. "Here we come."

Spyro sighed as the gremlin disappeared through the doors. Well, it wasn't like Kaos didn't know they were standing on his front doorstep.

That's what worried Spyro most of all.

* * *

The Kastle's entrance chamber was huge. A staircase rose up to a raised platform behind a massive golden statue of a particularly smug-looking Kaos. The Portal Master had obviously hoped that his likeness was imposing, but the effect was lessened by the fact that Trigger Happy was bouncing up and down on the evil Portal Master's bald head, blowing raspberries.

"Whoever designed this place was

bananas!" Food Fight said, whistling as he gazed up at the high-vaulted ceiling.

"No kidding," replied Terrafin. "Can it get any creepier?"

"Sure it can," said Cynder, pointing to a portrait on the wall. "Check out this guy."

Spyro couldn't help but snicker. The painting showed a young Kaos with a thick head of dark curly hair standing next to his long-suffering butler-turned-hench-Troll, Glumshanks.

"Who would have thought that Kaos looked worse with hair?" Cynder said with a smirk.

"I'M SO GLAD I AMUSE YOU, SKYLOSER!" thundered a voice that seemed to come from every angle.

"THIS IS THE VOICE OF KAOS," the voice continued, although there was no mistaking the Portal Master's nasal whine, even at this volume. "YOU DARE ENTER MY DOMAIN, FOOLS?"

"Yeah, we dare," Spyro shouted back.

"And we dare to kick your butt, too," Terrafin

added, shrugging when he received a long, hard glare from the purple dragon. "What?"

Spyro rolled his eyes before turning his attention back to the disembodied voice. "Show yourself, Kaos. Or are you too scared to face us?"

Kaos's voice laughed so much that it almost dissolved into a coughing fit. "ME? SCARED OF YOU? HA! HAVE YOU EVER HEARD ANYTHING SOOOO RIDICULOUS, GLUMSHANKS?"

Another voice joined the conversation. This one was even whinier, if such a thing were possible.

"No, Lord Kaos. Although there was that one time in—"

"SIIIIILENCE!" Kaos boomed. "I ASSUME YOU HAVE COME FOR THE MASK? MY MASK! TELL ME, HOW IS HUGO? STILL FEELING"— Kaos paused to snicker—"SHEEPISH?"

"What are you trying to do?" Lightning Rod shouted. "Bore us into submission? Come out and face us like the worm you are!"

There was more laughter at this. This time it was so loud that the foundations trembled and dust fell from the ceiling.

"FACE YOU, YOU SAY? WHAT A WONDERFUL IDEA! YOU WILL LEARN TO FEAR MY FEARSOME FACE, SKYFOOLS!"

"What does that even mean, Lord Kaos?" the Skylanders heard Glumshanks cut in. "I thought we'd discussed your lines."

"SHUT UP, IDIOT!" Kaos snapped, and the doors at the top of the stairwell crashed open by themselves. "YOU WANT THE MASK, SKYLANDERS? COME AND GET IT!"

"You heard the man," shouted Spyro, already racing up the thick-carpeted stairs. "We've got an arch-nemesis to defeat! Come on!"

Chapter Nine

The Mask of Power

It was like running through a maze. Corridors twisted in all directions, strange winged creatures flapped overhead, and flaming torches cast strange shadows against the walls. Kaos's cruel voice taunted them at every turn.

"THAT'S RIGHT, SKYLOSERS. GETTING WARMER! COME AND FIND ME. BWA-HA-HA-HAAAA!"

"I'm looking forward to making him eat his words," muttered Spyro.

"As long as he eats my veggies first," said Food Fight, sprinting beside the dragon.

Trigger Happy, meanwhile, was just shouting "Pow, pow, pow!" over and over as he scurried ahead.

After a while, the corridors all started to blur into one. Spyro began to suspect that they were running around in circles.

"No, look!" yelled Trigger Happy as they skidded around a corner to reveal an arch up ahead.

"That's got to be it!" cried Smolderdash.

"Only one way to find out," said Food Fight.

The Skylanders barreled through the arch to find themselves standing on a balcony. Below them was a colossal room dominated by a ridiculously large throne. And in front of the throne . . .

"Kaos!" Trigger Happy shouted, not waiting for the others. Before Spyro could stop him, the Tech Skylander spat out his long tongue. It wrapped around a dusty chandelier, allowing Trigger Happy to swing down toward the evil Portal Master, firing coins all the while.

Kaos didn't even flinch. He just threw up his hands and hollered, "Invisible Wall of Unseeable Protection!"

THUMP!

It was like Trigger Happy had swung into a huge window. Spyro and the others winced as he flattened against the invisible wall and slid down to the floor with a painful squeak.

"Ow, ow, owwwww!"

"Is that the best you can do, FOOL-LANDERS?" Kaos cackled as Spyro and the others jumped over the balcony edge to surround the Portal Master.

"I wouldn't rile them up, master. There are an awful lot of them . . . ," pointed out Glumshanks, cowering behind his boss.

"Yeah, and only two of you!" Food Fight grinned, trying to decide who he would splat first.

"Indeed there are." Kaos grinned. "But I also have these!"

Kaos spread his hands wide, and the eight segments of the mask flew from his sleeves to spin in a large circle in front of him.

"The segments!" Spyro gasped.

"Thank you so much for collecting the last piece for me, Spyro," Kaos said with a sneer. "I couldn't have done it without you."

"That explains why you backed off," Smolderdash hissed. "Not because you were scared. You wanted the remaining segments in one place so you could send your Drow to steal them."

"Give hot stuff a medal!" Kaos laughed. "Handy little things, those shape-shifting pendants. I'll have to thank Auric for lending his to me . . . when I am LORD OF ALL!"

"That'll never happen," promised Spyro.

"Yeah," said Trigger Happy, who was still rubbing his squashed face. "We're gonna bring you down, down, down!"

"I'd like to see you try," Kaos said, "especially when I'm wearing this. Mask of

Power, I, KAOOOOOS, command you to restore yourself. Be one so that I may be ALL-POWERFUL!"

"Don't let him combine the segments, Skylanders," Spyro shouted. "Give him everything you've got! Now!"

If the storm Lightning Rod had summoned in the skies above Kaos's Kastle was noisy, it was nothing compared to the din caused by every Skylander attacking at once. There were golden coins and Solar Orbs, exploding fruit and bolts of lightning. Fists pounded, horns butted, and mallets stomped, but nothing even dented Kaos's invisible barrier.

As Glumshanks rammed his fingers into his big flappy ears, the eight segments of the mask came together in front of Kaos's face. The individual pieces glowed with terrible power and merged—eight becoming one.

"Behold!" Kaos shrieked. "The Mask of Power, whole again."

"Spyro, he's done it!" Trigger Happy

shouted as the completed Mask hung in the air.

"Stop him before he puts it on!" Spyro cried out, but it was too late. The mask shot backward, slapping into Kaos's face all by itself. As the Skylanders watched in horror, the wood molded itself to their enemy's features. The Portal Master's body began to grow to twice its normal size. Even Glumshanks looked scared.

"Yes!" Kaos hissed. "This is the moment I've been waiting for! The moment when I finally meet my destiny. The moment that I receive the POWER OF THE MASK."

As the villain spoke, Trigger Happy looked down at his own fur. "Huh? Why am I glowing?"

Spyro glanced around. It wasn't just Trigger Happy. "We're all glowing!"

"Bet you didn't expect that, eh, DRAGONFLY?" Kaos jeered, now floating in the air before them.

"What's happening?" asked Food Fight as the glow from the Skylanders intensified. It felt like they were being pulled apart.

"I . . . don't . . . like . . . it!" screamed Trigger Happy as his glow abruptly left his body, streaked away from him, and shot into the air like a crazy firefly. The same thing happened to each Skylander in the room, until the air was buzzing with eerie, luminous globes.

Smolderdash fell to her knees. "I feel so weak," she said with a gasp.

"Me too," said Spyro, almost unable to stand.

Kaos stuck out his wooden bottom lip, the Mask of Power having now completely

merged with his face. "*Awwwww*, do the little Skylanders feel unwell? TOO BAD! I feel GREEEEEAT!"

The first of the flying lights darted forward, breaking through the invisible barrier and smashing into Kaos's hovering body.

"YES!" he shouted as the others followed suit. With each light that Kaos absorbed, the Portal Master glowed brighter and brighter.

"Spyro? What do we do? He's got us beet!" Food Fight said, but the purple dragon was too dazed to reply.

"What's the matter? Chompy got your tongue?" Kaos thundered. "Here, let me loosen it for you!"

Kaos opened his mouth and breathed out a column of flame. It took all of Spyro's effort to roll out of the way just in time.

"Can't stand the heat, huh?" Kaos grinned. "What about you, Smolderdash?"

As the Fire Skylander watched the scene openmouthed, Kaos summoned a trio of familiar fiery balls out of thin air.

"My Solar Orbs," she gasped.

"Oh, you want them back?" Kaos laughed. "HERE!"

Kaos lobbed the flaming orbs at Smolderdash, only missing the Fire Skylander because Food Fight knocked her out of the way. The Life Skylander rolled and came up ready to fire his fruit cannon. Food Fight pulled the trigger and—

CLICK.

That was it. No tomatoes. No zucchini. No fruit or vegetables at all.

"It must have jammed," Food Fight muttered, slapping the barrel against his hand.

"No, it's worse than that," Spyro said as Kaos threw an exploding pot of gold into the crowd of Skylanders.

"Those are our weapons!" Trigger Happy spluttered, ducking out of the way of the blast.

"Yeah," Spyro said. "Kaos has stolen our powers!"

Chapter Ten

Skylands' Darkest Hour

"This is AMAZING!" Kaos shrieked, juggling a crop of fresh tomatoes that had appeared from nowhere. He was standing on a cloud that looked very much like Lightning Rod's—much to the annoyance of the Storm Titan.

"Give that back!" the big blue hero called out, but it was to no avail. He could barely raise his fists, let alone throw a lightning bolt.

Standing in front of the Skylanders, Trigger Happy raised his golden guns with shaking hands. The invisible barrier was gone now. Kaos was too powerful to need protection.

"Big mistake," Trigger Happy whispered to himself as he aimed. "Enormous mistake."

Closing one of his yellow eyes to take aim, Trigger Happy fired, and his golden pistols spat a pair of shining coins.

"Going to hit you right between the . . ."

Trigger Happy's voice trailed off, his jaw dropped, and his tongue unfurled. No, that wasn't possible. As he gaped, the coins flew wide and embedded themselves in the stone pillars behind the villainous Portal Master.

"Oops," said Kaos. "Missed!"

"But I never miss," muttered Trigger Happy. "Never, never, never!"

"Neither do I!" Kaos smirked, holding up a lightning bolt in one hand and a Solar Orb in the other. As he spoke, giant curved horns grew out of his already transformed head, and an army of ghosts shimmered into existence behind him.

"Not my ghosts, too!" Cynder moaned as Kaos threw his first lightning bolt. It screamed down toward the ailing Skylanders, and there was nothing they could do to stop it. Trigger Happy was still staring at his guns in disbelief, Smolderdash's light had gone out, and Spyro could hardly stand. After all their battles, after all their victories, the Skylanders were finished.

"NO!"

The voice echoed around the Kastle, strong and defiant. It was accompanied by a flash of light. At first Smolderdash thought that the lightning bolt had hit, but when the glare faded she realized they weren't in Kaos's Kastle anymore.

"There you are," someone said in a small, friendly voice. "Thank goodness that you're safe."

The Skylanders looked up to see Hugo scampering toward them.

Food Fight glanced around. "We're back in the Portal Room. In the Citadel."

"Indeed you are, my Skylanders," said the voice they'd heard in Kaos's lair. Master Eon was standing next to the Portal of Power, leaning heavily on the stone platform.

"You summoned us back with the Portal?" Trigger Happy asked.

"All of us at the same time?" Smolderdash added. "But that's . . ."

"Tiring. Yes, it is," admitted the Portal Master. He tried to smile weakly, but even that seemed too much effort. "But I couldn't leave you there, in Kaos's clutches."

Spyro pushed himself to his feet and padded forward. "Master Eon, Kaos . . ." He faltered, unable to bring himself to say the words.

"Kaos has stolen your powers. Every last one."

"It was the mask," Food Fight said. "As soon as he put it on . . ."

Master Eon nodded. "I know. Finally we know the secret of the Mask of Power."

Hugo's eyes went wide behind his thick glasses as he realized what Master Eon meant. "The ancient scrolls, they say that the mask makes its wearer all-powerful, but that's not the case, is it?"

"I'm afraid not," Master Eon said. "It appears that the mask doesn't make you all-powerful. Instead, it lets you steal all the powers."

"All the powers of the Skylanders!" Trigger Happy gasped.

"So that's how he did it," Spyro spluttered. "As long as he wears the mask . . ."

"He can use your abilities against you," Master Eon confirmed. "It seems even Nefarion didn't understand the mask's true potential."

"But what about the others?" asked Food Fight. "Yeah, he stole our powers, but there are lots of other Skylanders besides us."

"It's no good," said Hugo sadly. "You'd better come outside and see."

Without another word, the librarian led the weary Skylanders into the lush grounds that stretched out beneath the Core of Light.

"Oh no!" Spyro gasped. "It can't be."

But it was. The lawn was covered with the rest of the Skylanders, each looking as tired as Spyro felt. Pop Fizz looked frazzled,

Fright Rider had given up the ghost, and Sonic Boom wheezed, having completely lost her voice. Worst of all was Eruptor, who was shivering violently. His usually red-hot skin was blue—the living lava that ran through his veins had frozen solid.

"So c-c-c-cold," he stammered, his teeth chattering. "Has someone g-g-got a b-blanket?"

Spyro tried to breathe some fire to warm his friend, but instead could only hack up a small wisp of smoke.

"This is hopeless," said Smolderdash, feeling a chill herself for the first time in her life. "How can we defeat Kaos without our powers?"

"No," Master Eon insisted, striking the end of his staff against the ground in frustration. "There is always hope. We'll find a way." The Portal Master glanced up at the Core of Light, the tall beacon that kept The Darkness at bay. "We simply have to."

Chapter Eleven

Ultimate Kaos

It wasn't long before news of Kaos's antics started to spread. It appeared that the evil Portal Master was practicing his newfound skills whenever possible.

The first attack happened on Oilspill Island. Gillmen were setting out for a day with their nets when a giant figure came skating across the ocean on a surfboard made of ice. Before the Gillmen could paddle back to shore, they were trapped in ice prisons that bobbed around in the sea.

"Frozen fishy fools!" Kaos cheered, before teleporting away. "Have an ICE day!"

Later that same morning, the forest folk of Treetop Terrace were minding their own business when Kaos dropped down from above. As the Treemen ran for shelter, the Portal Master turned his attention to the trees themselves.

"I've never trusted you," he ranted. "Standing there all leafy and still. I know you've been plotting against me all along. In fact, you've been driving me NUTS!"

Without further warning, Kaos spat a huge, spiky acorn at the nearest tree, which exploded on impact.

"SERVES YOU RIGHT, YOU LEAFY FOOL!" Kaos screamed, before proceeding to make a new clearing in the middle of the forest, just for the fun of it.

Next, Kaos swept into the Frostfest Mountains. The yetis living there thought they were ready for anything, but never expected to have a wicked Portal Master spew boiling-hot magma all over their alpine villages. Even their ice cream sundaes melted, which was Kaos's real goal (it's a little-known fact that he has always resented the yetis for refusing to share their ice-cream recipe with him).

Back at the Citadel, the Skylanders' moods darkened with every new report.

"We need to stop him," grumbled Smolderdash.

"But how?" Food Fight said, his hopes

squashed. "Without our powers, we're helpless."

"No!" Spyro said forcefully. The more he'd listened to the news about Kaos's exploits, the more he'd scowled. Now, he'd had enough. "We're Skylanders! We're never helpless and we never give up!"

Trigger Happy didn't comment. He just aimed his golden pistols at the Citadel walls—and still managed to miss!

"See?" Food Fight said. "Even Trigger Happy can't shoot straight."

"So?" Spyro asked. "Our powers may be gone, but we're more than just our abilities." He thumped a claw against his scaly chest. "It's what's in here that counts. Do we want to see Kaos win?"

"No," the Skylanders murmured.

"Do we want to protect Skylands?"

"Yes!" they responded, louder now.

"Are we ready to quit?"

"NO!" Spyro's friends yelled back.

"So, what do we do?" Trigger Happy

asked, almost jumping up and down with his usual enthusiasm.

Spyro looked up at the towering beacon above them. "Kaos is still experimenting with the powers he stole from us, learning how to use them. But soon he'll come after the Core of Light."

Master Eon had been sitting in the shade of a tree, quietly watching Spyro rouse his fellow Skylanders, but now he stood up and spoke. "I have no doubt of that, Spyro. The Core is the only thing that can stop him from spreading The Darkness across Skylands."

"And do you think he can destroy it?" asked Food Fight.

"With the amount of power he's wielding?" Master Eon replied. "It's certainly possible. Thanks to the Mask of Power, he can tap into all eight of the known Elements. Such power hasn't been seen in Skylands for millennia. Who knows what he can do?"

"So we have to act," Spyro said, flying above the heads of the assembled Skylanders, which took more effort than usual. "We need to prepare ourselves so we're ready when Kaos comes knocking! Are you with me?"

"We're with you, Spyro," responded Smolderdash, speaking for them all. "What do you want us to do?"

Spyro grinned. "We're going to build a wall!"

Chapter Twelve

Protecting the Core

Kaos was having the time of his life. He swooped through the clouds, diving and looping. He'd flown before, of course, but only in machines and hot-air balloons. This was different. This was exhilarating.

Glumshanks, on the other hand, was having a less than wonderful time. The Troll was hanging on to his master's back, eyes closed tight, hoping that he'd feel solid ground beneath his flat feet very soon. Not that he was foolish enough to complain. Last time he'd moaned, Kaos had tried out Double Trouble's power on him, creating an army of little Kaos clones who ran up to Glumshanks and exploded in his face.

"This is amazing, Glumshanks," Kaos exclaimed, vaporizing a passing flying fish with a lightning bolt just because he could. "I've never felt so powerful."

"And I've never felt so airsick!"

"What was that, FOOL?"

"I said, 'You've learned to use your powers so quick, sir.' It's amazing."

Satisfied, Kaos nodded. "Yes, I am pretty wonderful. I think the time has come, Glumshanks!"

"For us to land?" the Troll asked hopefully.

"No, you coward!" Kaos snapped. "For us to attack the Core of Light!"

"Should we call in the Drow to help, sir?" Glumshanks asked. "Or maybe your Troll armies?"

"Who, those IDIOTS?" Kaos crowed, swooping around the peak of a towering mountain three times, just for fun. "Like I, KAOOOOOOS, need them! Remember, I am Kaos the All-Powerful now, Glumshanks."

"As if you'd let me forget," Glumshanks muttered under his breath.

"What did you say?"

"That you'd destroy the Core of Light, no sweat, sir," Glumshanks quickly replied.

"Indeed I shall, Glumshanks," Kaos declared, his narrow chest plumping up with pride. "Nothing can stand in my way this time. Not Eon. Not that pathetic band of SKYLOSERS. No one! Skylands is mine! Skylands is DOOOOOMED!"

Kaos was still cackling with glee when Master Eon's island came into view.

"There it is, Glumshanks," the fiendish Portal Master yelled. "My destiny awaits!"

The Troll peered over his master's shoulder. "But where is the Core of Light?" Glumshanks asked.

Kaos snickered. "Foolish fool, it's right there, beside Eon's accursed Cita—"

His voice trailed off. Glumshanks was indeed a foolish fool, but on this occasion he was a correct fool, too. Where the Core of Light should have been, there now stood what looked very much like a tall wooden tower.

"What have they done?" Kaos gasped.

On the island, Spyro looked up at the tower and nodded in appreciation.

"Well done, everyone," he said. "We did it!"

"Yeah, yeah, yeah!" said Trigger Happy, knocking in one last nail with a golden hammer. "Bang, bang, bang!"

They'd worked all night, with Master Eon bringing in wood from all across Skylands through the Portal. Sprocket, the mechanically gifted Tech Skylander, had sketched out the plans in the dirt, and the Skylanders had sawed planks, hammered nails, and tightened screws. The result looked a little precarious, but they'd managed to build a circular tower all around the Core of Light, shielding it from attack—at least that was the plan.

Best of all, they'd done it using good old-fashioned hard work. No powers, no potions—just a lot of effort and cooperation. Spyro had never been so proud of his friends.

"I've seen sturdier-looking celery. Are you sure it's going to hold?" Food Fight asked, scratching the back of his head. The tower hadn't looked so rickety in Sprocket's drawings.

"Well, we're about to find out," said Smolderdash, pointing to the sky. "Look!"

The Skylanders spun around to see heavy

black clouds rolling toward them. Thunder rumbled on the horizon, and a terrible wind was blowing. The tower was already creaking ominously.

Beside Master Eon, Hugo fished a telescope out of his backpack, snapped it open, and peered into the middle of the clouds.

"It's h-h-him," the Mabu stammered, the telescope trembling in his hands. "It's K-Kaos."

There was no time to lose. "Battle stations!" Spyro shouted, and the Skylanders scrambled into action. It was time for phase two of the plan.

As well as building the wall around the Core, the Skylanders had constructed a dozen large catapults.

"Load 'em up!" yelled Trigger Happy, hopping about in excitement. Around him, the largest Skylanders were clambering into the catapults—Prism Break, Terrafin, Stump Smash, Slobber Tooth, and more. These catapults wouldn't fire rocks or boulders.

They would fire Skylanders!

"Get ready!" Spyro commanded as Kaos zoomed nearer and nearer. "This is it!"

Everyone fell silent as they waited for the order to fire. All except Trigger Happy, that is.

"Can I have a go, Spyro? Can I? Can I?"

Spyro shook his head. "No, Trigger Happy. We've talked about this. You're too light. We need to throw our heaviest Skylanders at Kaos to slow him down. I need you here with me."

Trigger Happy muttered unhappily as Master Eon walked to the front of the collected Skylanders and raised his staff toward the incoming fiend. The crystal at the end of the rod began to glow.

"Kaos!" Eon boomed, his voice magically amplified. "Come no farther!"

In the sky above the island, Kaos came to a sudden stop, and Glumshanks only just managed to stop himself from being thrown off his back.

"Ha!" the evil Portal Master shouted down. "You can't stop me, Eon. Not this time. Your SKYBLUNDERERS are helpless, and you are DOOMED!"

Master Eon clicked his tongue. "You were always such a boring conversationalist, Kaos. Doomed this and doomed that. Why don't you scurry back to your lair and learn some new threats?"

"And why don't you buzz off and wash your beard, old man? This is between me and the Skylanders," Kaos replied, not taking the bait for once. "And don't think that pathetic tower will stop me. I am INVINCIBLE!"

"This is your last warning, Kaos," Master Eon said calmly. "Leave now, while you still can."

Kaos's only response was an evil cackle—oh, and the electrified breath he'd stolen from Cynder. The villainous Portal Master arched his back and opened his mouth wide, breathing a stream of dark energy that crackled down toward Master Eon. It would have hit him, too, if Spyro hadn't hurled himself up and knocked his mentor out of the way.

"Master Eon, look out!"

"I am fine, Spyro," Master Eon replied sadly as smoke curled up from where the electric breath had struck. "But it seems Kaos is unwilling to listen to reason."

"As always," Spyro said, turning to the Skylanders. "First wave, FIRE!"

THWAP!

The first three catapults fired, flinging Terrafin, Stump Smash, and Slobber Tooth

into the great blue yonder. The three bulky Skylanders rocketed toward Kaos.

"L-L-Lord Kaos!" babbled Glumshanks. "What are we going to do?"

"Oh, just this," said Kaos, as if he didn't have a care in the world. He knocked Terrafin out of the sky with a handful of exploding fruit.

"And this!" A blast of rainbow energy sent Slobber Tooth flying.

"And, of course, THIS!" A wall of flame rushed toward Stump Smash, sending him spinning back down to the ground.

Below the battle, Trigger Happy was still nagging Spyro. "Now can I have a go? Please, please, *pleeeease*?"

"No!" Spyro insisted, turning to the catapults. "Second wave, prepare to fire!"

But Trigger Happy hadn't hung around for Spyro's answer. He was sprinting over to where Lightning Rod was waiting to catapult himself into action.

"Rod, Rod, Rod," Trigger Happy said. "Isn't that a picture of you?"

"What? Where?" said the Storm Titan, whose ego was almost as large as his biceps. "I hope they got my good side."

Without thinking, Lightning Rod leaped out of the catapult to look for the picture, giving Trigger Happy the chance to scramble in. Before Rod realized what was happening, the gutsy gremlin had released the counterweight.

"Trigger Happy," the Storm Titan bellowed. "Wait!"

THWOP!

The catapult fired, propelling Trigger Happy into the sky.

Chapter Thirteen

Rain of Terror

"Wahoo!" whooped Trigger Happy as he *whooshed* toward Kaos. The wind rushed through his fur and, for a second, he felt indestructible. Hoisting his golden pistols above his head, he rattled off gold coins and prepared to barge straight into the Portal Master.

In front of him, Glumshanks was shivering in fear, pointing out Trigger Happy to his master—but Trigger Happy didn't mind. There was no way he could miss. Not this time.

WHOOSH!

The Tech Skylander shot past Kaos and

into the swirling clouds.

He'd missed! Again!

"No, no, no!"

Trigger Happy could hear Kaos laughing as he rocketed into the heavens. He had no idea how to stop—or get back to the battle. It wasn't fair—they'd all be having a blast down there!

"A blast!" Trigger Happy shouted. That was it! He screwed up his eyes, visualizing one of his pots of gold. He just needed a small one to blast him back down to the ground.

"Just! One! Small! Pot!"

The fuzzy gremlin opened his eyes to reveal . . . nothing. He sighed, hardly even registering the fact that his flight path was now arcing downward. He was tumbling between the islands and would fall a long, long way.

A sudden beat of leathery wings caused Trigger Happy to snap up his head. Something was zooming in toward him. No, not something—someone!

"Spyro!" Trigger Happy cried out happily

as his purple friend swooped down, claws outstretched.

"I've got you," wheezed Spyro, hooking his claws under Trigger Happy's arms. Effort was apparent all over the dragon's face, the strain of flying in his weakened condition obvious, but Spyro hadn't been about to let his friend fall.

"What were you thinking?" Spyro hissed through clenched fangs as they came about, gliding back to Master Eon's island.

"Pow, pow, pow!" was Trigger Happy's only reply.

Spyro nodded. "You wanted to stop Kaos, I know. We all do! But don't you remember what I said? We have to work together—especially now."

"Yeah, Spyro," Trigger Happy replied meekly—or as meekly as he ever got. "Sorry!"

Spyro grunted as he flapped his wings. "Besides, we're going to need as much help as we can get down there on the ground!"

Kaos landed in the middle of the Skylanders with a crash, shaking the very earth.

"Mind if I drop in, FOOLS?" He sneered as a wall of bone brambles, bamboo sticks, and thorns burst out of the grass around him, shielding him instantly from the powerless Skylanders.

From within his protective circle, he fired lightning bolts, fireballs, and even a swarm of honeybees at the Skylanders.

Cynder tried to fly over the defenses, only to find herself attacked by a pack of spooky ghosts—her own spooky ghosts.

"See how you like it for a change, dragon!" Kaos shouted. "And now for that tower!"

He threw his hands into the air. "I, KAOOS, summon fire from the sky! Oh, and stars and skulls, too!"

The Skylanders scattered as Kaos's rain of terror started to fall. Flaming balls, shining stars, and grinning skulls tumbled down, falling

straight into the Skylanders' makeshift tower.

Spyro and Trigger Happy swooped down just as the curved wooden walls started to shatter. Planks were thrown into the air, and nails pinged from the woodwork.

Within seconds, all their hard work was undone. The tower crashed to the ground, revealing the Core of Light in all its glory. It shined brightly into the darkening sky—but for how much longer?

"At last!" Kaos screeched. "Nothing can stop me now! NOTHING!"

"Is that so?" boomed a voice, clear and sharp despite the sound of the falling tower. Behind the Skylanders, Master Eon raised his staff and slammed it into the ground like a pile driver. The impact sent a crack snaking toward Kaos and the clearly terrified Glumshanks. The shockwave hit Kaos's protective circle, and the thorns, bones, and bamboo tubes crumbled to dust, revealing the evil Portal Master.

"Eon!" Kaos hissed. "You don't stand a chance against me. Not when I wear the MASK OF POWER!"

"Not when you hide behind it, you mean," Master Eon roared, a bolt of energy flashing toward his rival. Kaos raised his palm, and a huge toadstool erupted from the ground in front of him, easily absorbing the blow.

"Is that the best you can do?" Kaos cackled, leaping into the air, flipping head-over-heels, and smashing into the ground. As Glumshanks ran for cover, Kaos burrowed beneath the earth, disappearing from view. The ground trembled as he tunneled below the Skylanders' feet, planning to burst out of the soil and smash into Master Eon.

Instead, he sailed through Master Eon as if the old wizard were a ghost.

"What?" Kaos said, whirling around as the duplicate of Eon faded from view. The real Portal Master, standing on the other side of the island, muttered a spell beneath his breath, and vines erupted from the ground, wrapping themselves around Kaos's arms and legs.

"Ha!" Kaos jeered. "These couldn't hold a Wilikin!" In a flash, he had burned the vines to a crisp. "Don't you get it, Eon? Anything you can do"—he clapped his hands together, and vines sprouted around Eon's legs—"I can do better, FOOL!"

Master Eon struggled, but it was too late. The vines were multiplying, new shoots growing at an alarming rate. Within seconds, the Portal Master's arms were bound, and his staff had fallen from his hand.

"Master Eon!" Spyro cried out, running forward. In the time it took for the dragon to reach his mentor's side, Eon was completely smothered.

His body, his head—even his beard. All that was visible of the good Portal Master was two sharp eyes staring out from the green prison.

"Take one more step," Kaos warned the purple dragon, "and I'll blow Eon sky-high."

Spyro gasped as glistening green melons bloomed on the vines holding Master Eon. *Highly explosive* glistening green melons.

"And the same goes for any of you, SKYLOSERS," Kaos added. "Stay exactly where you are. In fact, FREEZE!"

Spyro and Trigger Happy shivered as ice blocks appeared around their feet, anchoring them in place. Slowly, the ice started to creep up their legs. The same thing was happening to the other Skylanders, too. Soon, all of them would be completely covered in ice.

"Excellent," Kaos said smugly. "And while you're cooling down, I'll do what I came here to do—DESTROY THE CORE OF LIGHT, FOREVER! HA-HA-HA-HAAAAAAAA!"

Chapter Fourteen

Kaos the All-Powerful

Kaos's eyes flashed with diabolical fire as balls of pure energy crackled in the middles of his palms, brighter than the Core of Light itself.

This is it, thought Trigger Happy. *He really is going to do it this time. Kaos is going to destroy the Core of Light.*

All around, the Skylanders were struggling against their ice prisons, unable to break free.

But Spyro said we could beat Kaos if we worked together, Trigger Happy thought— and an idea hit him like a gold coin striking a bull's-eye. That was it. Working together!

"Hey, Kaos!" the Tech Skylander shouted. "I bet you think you're pretty smart stealing our powers, huh?"

Kaos paused, a look of amusement crossing his face. He'd never heard Trigger Happy string together such a long sentence. No one had.

"You think you're *sooooooooo* powerful. So awesome!"

Kaos smirked. "Yes, I am. I am the most powerful being ever to walk Skylands, FOOL!"

"Yeah?" Trigger Happy grinned. "Bet you still can't fire straight."

"Of course I can!" Kaos bridled.

"Prove it!" Trigger Happy challenged. "Take one of my golden guns!"

Kaos gestured toward the Core of Light. "You realize that I'm a little busy here? I have to—"

"Destroy the Core. Yeah, yeah, yeah, we know." Trigger Happy rolled his eyes. "We're doomed. You're the greatest. Blah, blah, blah."

"Riiiiight. Well, do you mind if I finish?" Kaos asked, hands on hips.

"See, Spyro?" Trigger Happy said to the dragon beside him. "I told you he couldn't fire my guns."

"Trigger Happy, what are you doing?" Spyro whispered to the gold-slinging gremlin.

"Just follow my lead," Trigger Happy hissed back.

"I could fire your guns if I wanted to," Kaos snapped.

"Don't believe you!" Trigger Happy shot back. "I bet you can't!"

"I bet I can," said Kaos, incensed.

"Can't! Can't! Can't!" Trigger Happy giggled.

"Can! Can! Can!" Kaos replied.

Spyro picked up the chant. "Can't! Can't! Can't!"

Even through the mask, the Skylanders could tell Kaos's face was starting to turn red. "Shut up!"

The rest of the Skylanders joined in. "Can't! Can't! Can't!"

"SILENCE!" Kaos bellowed. "I'll show you all!"

He raised a clawed hand, and Trigger Happy's guns started to shake inside the ice block.

"Can't! Can't! Can't! Can't! Can't! Can't!"

With an earsplitting crack, the guns spun out of the ice, freeing Trigger Happy in the process. As the pistols slapped into Kaos's waiting hands, Trigger Happy started running among the trapped Skylanders.

"Now we'll see who can fire straight," sneered the Portal Master. "Stand still when I'm trying to shoot you!"

Trigger Happy weaved in and out of the ice prisons. "Oh, firing a few gold coins is easy. Pow, pow, pow!" He paused by Smolderdash. "What about doing it while burning brighter than a sun?"

"You mean like this?" Kaos smirked, his body starting to glow with Smolderdash's power.

Trigger Happy was over by Food Fight now. "That's okay, I guess. But it would be a lot more impressive if you were sitting on a giant revolving tomato!"

"Like THIS ONE?" cried Kaos, a humongous red tomato appearing beneath him.

"And breathing fire!" Spyro chipped in, immediately prompting smoke to curl out of Kaos's mouth.

All around the field, the other Skylanders realized what Trigger Happy was up to.

"Do it while burping lava!" Eruptor shouted.

"And spitting acorns!" added Stump Smash.

"And controlling the weather!" bellowed Lightning Rod.

"And calling up ghosts!" said Cynder.

Kaos reacted to every challenge. He

coughed up magma and exploding nuts. He caused rain clouds to form overhead and whipped up a gaggle of giggling ghosts. And still the calls kept coming.

"Create sea slime!"

"Fire your Bambazooker!"

"Generate ice armor!"

"Summon animal spirits!"

"Shoot crystal shards!"

"Turn into a tornado!"

"DO! IT! ALL!" Trigger Happy shouted, leaping up and down.

In front of them, Kaos was in trouble. Spurred on by the Skylanders, he was trying to use all their powers at the same time—something no one person was supposed to do, Mask of Power or no Mask of Power.

"I can do this!" he cried out, although his voice trembled with fear. "I am SUPREME!"

"Lord Kaos, stop!" Glumshanks yelled from his hiding place, before running toward his master, who was trying to do dozens of things at once. "It's a trick! The Skylanders are . . . AAARGH!"

The Troll was knocked from his feet by Kaos's flame whip, which was flailing around like a crazed snake.

"HELP . . . ME!" Kaos screamed, his voice louder than Sonic Boom's cry. Prism Break's crystals were forming and shattering across his back, his arms burning up like Hot Dog's. "I can't stop it! I CAN'T STOP IT!"

Trigger Happy's grin was wider than ever. "No, but I can!" he said, and he stuck out his incredibly long tongue.

Chapter Fifteen

Unmasked

Trigger Happy's tongue flicked toward Kaos, slapping the Mask of Power. With a twist of his head—and using his super-sticky saliva—Trigger Happy yanked the mask right off the Portal Master's face.

The effect was instantaneous. In fact, it might have happened even faster than that. Free from Kaos's face, the mask snapped back to its original shape. Lights burst from the evil Portal Master's body. They raced around the sky like the best fireworks show you've ever seen and then found their homes. The Skylanders' powers returned to them, one by one.

In turn, the Skylanders smashed their ice prisons, feeling stronger than ever before. The Citadel's gardens filled with their battle cries.

"A blaze of glory!"

"One strike and you're out!"

"Fear the fish!"

"Born to burn!"

"All fired up!"

"NOOOOOOOOOO!" Kaos wailed, falling to his knees.

"YESSSS!" Trigger Happy replied, catching the Mask of Power in his hand.

"It's all mine, mine, mine!"

"Good work, Trigger Happy!" cried Spyro, but the smile soon fell from his scaly face. Trigger Happy was standing in the midst of the Skylanders, staring intently at the mask. As Spyro watched, it looked like Trigger Happy was actually considering putting it on!

"No, Trigger Happy! Don't!" Spyro cried. But Trigger Happy smiled, winking at the dragon.

"Of course I won't!" the Tech Skylander said, flicking out his tongue to retrieve his golden guns and throwing the Mask of Power high into the sky at the same time.

"This thing's history. Three, two, one— FIRE!"

Working together, the Skylanders threw everything they had at the wooden mask. Fire. Ice. Water. Magic. Lightning. And, of course, golden coins. They all hit their mark, and the Mask of Power exploded into a million tiny

pieces—far too many to ever put together again.

"My beautiful mask!" Kaos bawled, but it was too late. The defeated Portal Master's eyes dropped, and he found himself surrounded by every single Skylander.

"L-L-Lord Kaos, I think we should leave," Glumshanks gulped, trying to help his master to his feet.

"A good idea," said Eon from behind the crowd of Skylanders. The Portal Master had been freed, the vines and exploding fruit having withered away to nothing as soon as Kaos's stolen powers were lost. The Skylanders parted to let Master Eon pass.

"The Mask of Power is destroyed, and Skylands is safe once more. And as for you"—Master Eon pointed his staff at the cringing villain—"you need to be taught a lesson, once and for all!" The crystal on the end of the staff began to glow, and Kaos threw up his hands to ward off Master Eon's magic.

"NOOOO!" Kaos screeched as a ball of light plucked him and Glumshanks from the ground. "You may have won today, Eon! But I, KAOOOOS, shall return, and then you shall see how *baaaaaaaaaaaaad* I am."

Spyro snickered. "What was that, Kaos?"

Kaos opened his mouth to reply but could only manage a surprised bleat.

"Turn my librarian into a sheep, will you?" Master Eon said. "Let's see how the two of you like it!"

In front of the amazed Skylanders, Kaos and Glumshanks started spinning around and around, faster and faster. Finally the ball of light popped, leaving two startled sheep suspended in midair.

"Ha!" Food Fight laughed. "Like peas in a pod!"

There was one difference, though. The sheep on the left was covered in coarse black wool, while the one on the right was decidedly green.

"No wonder they look so sheepish,"

Smolderdash said with a grin, "considering all the trouble they've caused."

"Yeah," agreed Spyro. "Maybe this'll give them a new *fleece* on life!"

Master Eon smiled, his staff still glowing, at the transformed tyrant and his *baaing* butler. "Trigger Happy, are you ready to send them home?"

"Yeah, yeah, yeah!" gabbled the Skylander, sliding an explosive pot of gold underneath the sheep's frantically scrabbling legs. "Blam, blam, *lamb!*"

BANG!

The pot detonated, sending the two sheep flying into the air and far away from the Citadel. As the Skylanders watched them go, they were sure they heard Kaos scream one final warning:

"I'll be *baaaaaaaaaaaaaaack!*"

The Skylanders cheered, but Spyro noticed that Food Fight was staring thoughtfully into the sky.

"What's up?"

"That fruit-loop means it, doesn't he?" the Life Skylander said. "No matter how many times we defeat Kaos, he always comes back!"

"Yeah, but we're always waiting for him," Spyro said with a smile. "Right, Trigger Happy?"

Trigger Happy jumped onto the dragon's back and cheered as Spyro soared into the air. "Right! Skylanders united!" the Tech Skylander cried. "Pow! Pow! Pow!"

Far away, outside Kaos's foul Kastle, Kaos and Glumshanks tumbled from the sky. They landed in a woolly heap, and Master Eon's spell finally began to wear off. With a *pop*, their heads returned to normal . . . but their bottoms were still distinctly sheepish.

"I can't believe we lost—again!" Kaos said, tottering into the Kastle on his hooves. "It's your fault, of course, Glumshanks."

"Of course, sir," said the Troll, following

close behind. He'd probably be looking at a week or more in the dungeon for his part in Kaos's failure.

Suddenly, the evil Portal Master stopped short, and Glumshanks only just avoided barging into him.

"What is this?" Kaos asked, peering suspiciously at the large package that lay in the middle of the entrance hall. With a wiggle of his fingers, the package magically floated into the air and started to unwrap. Seconds later, the paper dropped to the floor to reveal . . .

"A book!" Kaos squealed, scampering forward. "And not just any book."

The Portal Master plucked the heavy-looking volume from the air. "I forgot I'd ordered this. You can keep your Books of Power—and your stupid masks, too! This is what we've been waiting for, Glumshanks!"

"What is it?" the Troll asked, peering over his master's shoulder. Kaos spun around, revealing the book's ominous title.

"*The Horrendous Horror of Hideous Horribleness?*" Glumshanks read, still none the wiser. "What in Skylands is that?"

"Victory!" Kaos hissed, hugging the book to his weedy chest and cackling the latest evil cackle in his long line of evil cackles. "Victory will be MIIINE!"

"Enjoy your undeserved glory while you can, SKYBLUNDERERS—because something wicked this way comes. Something really, really, really super wicked. You are all DOOOOOOOOOOOOOMED!"

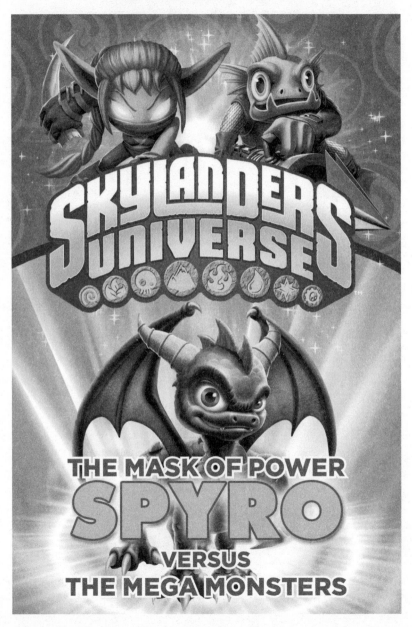

SKYLANDERS UNIVERSE

THE MASK OF POWER

GILL GRUNT

AND THE CURSE OF
THE FISH MASTER

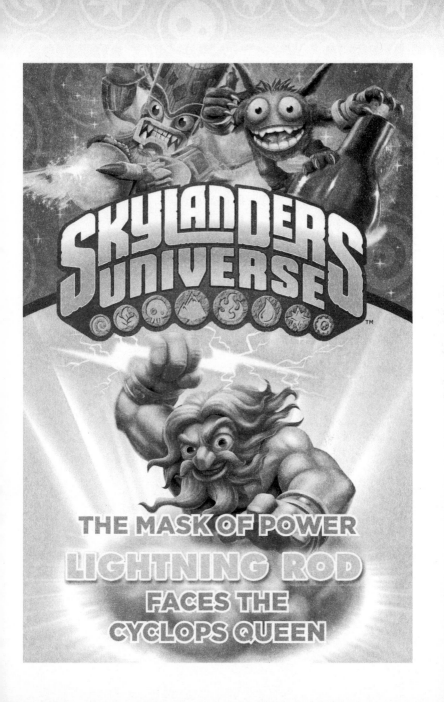

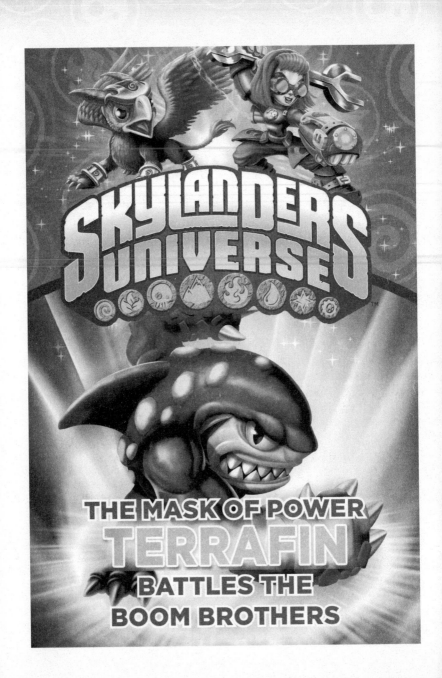

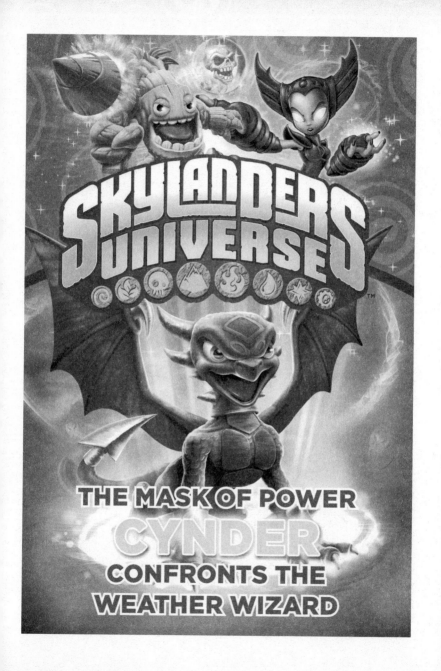

SKYLANDERS UNIVERSE

THE MASK OF POWER
CYNDER
CONFRONTS THE
WEATHER WIZARD

SKYLANDERS UNIVERSE

THE MASK OF POWER
STUMP SMASH
CROSSES THE
BONE DRAGON

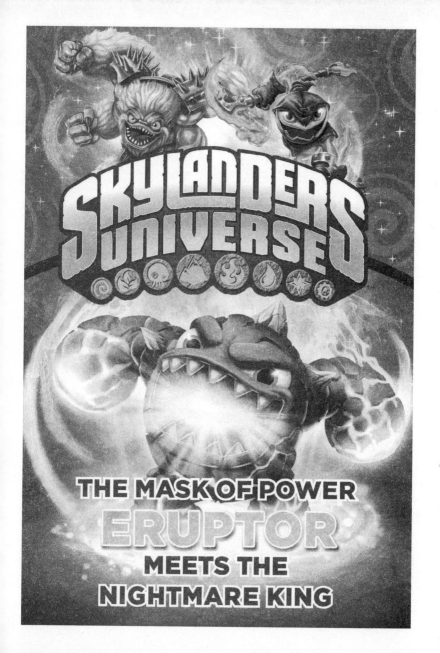

Also available:

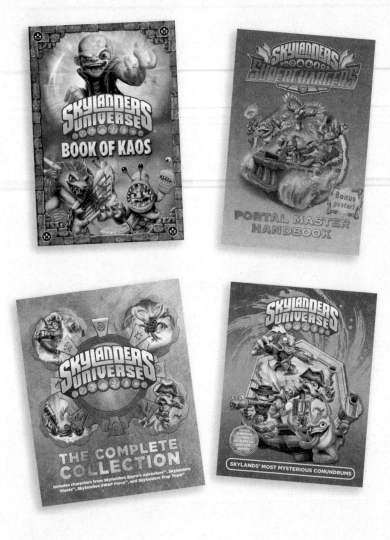